The Governesses

The Governesses

Anne Serre

translated from the French by Mark Hutchinson

A NEW DIRECTIONS PAPERBOOK ORIGINAL

Originally published in French as *Les gouvernantes* by Éditions Champ Vallon.

First published as New Directions Paperbook 1421 in 2018
Manufactured in the United States of America
New Directions Books are printed on acid-free paper
Design by Erik Rieselbach

Library of Congress Cataloging-in-Publication Data
Names: Serre, Anne, 1960– author. | Hutchinson, Mark, 1956– translator.
Title: The governesses / by Anne Serre ; translated by Mark Hutchinson.
Other titles: Gouvernantes. English
Description: New York : New Directions Publishing, 2018.
Identifiers: LCCN 2018021518 (print) | LCCN 2018024714 (ebook) | ISBN 9780811228084 (ebook) | ISBN 9780811228077 (acid-free paper)
Subjects: LCSH: Governesses—Fiction.
Classification: LCC PQ2679.E67335 (ebook) | LCC PQ2679.E67335 G6813 2018 (print) | DDC 843/.914—dc23
LC record available at https://lccn.loc.gov/2018021518

10 9 8 7 6 5 4 3 2 1

New Directions Books are published for James Laughlin
by New Directions Publishing Corporation
80 Eighth Avenue, New York 10011

The Governesses

THEIR HAIR HELD FIRMLY in place by black hairnets, they make their way along the path, talking together in the middle of a large garden. Around them, young boys frolic and prance around, chasing hoops under the trees. One of the two women holds a book to her chest. She has slipped a finger between the pages, and her chin is resting on the spine. Her head half-lowered, she has a dreamy air as she speaks. A gleam from her yellow leather ankle boots lashes the grass by the path, then jumps up like a startled hare. The other woman clasps two small valiant hands unencumbered by rings or bracelets, her only ornaments the ten pearl buttons that keep the sleeves of her blouse stretched tightly around her wrists.

Here they come, stepping up to the large white house. It's a low-roofed, two-story building, hidden away beneath high trees. Comfortably installed in the salon, they start gossiping with an almost stately air. They're like queens at this time of the year. The house is empty and they're preparing for a ball, it seems, the poor little fools—a ball in their own honor, and in honor of the little boys rolling hoops.

In the salon, the scene is scantily lit by a single small lamp on a card table at the center of the rug. From the outside you can see the shimmer of the young women's hair reflected in the French doors. They're hot, so they remove their brooches and scarves and unbutton their blouses. Tea is brought, which they drink by candlelight. Even in a state of semi-undress, they're a model of discretion, as smooth-skinned as infants fresh from the tub.

Eléonore appears to be reciting something. From the outside, you can see her lips move, at times quite forcefully. At other moments they remain parted for a spell. The gleam of her wet teeth is visible in the French doors.

While Eléonore talks, the other one stretches out comfortably on the settee, swinging her legs over the back then covering them at once with the skirt of her long dress. She eats pastries, snatching them up without looking as finger and thumb reach out at random across the low table, then closing her eyes as she carries them to her mouth.

These are the governesses. Tomorrow, the family will be back: Monsieur and Madame Austeur, Monsieur and Madame Austeur's four children, and the little maids, plus one or two friends perhaps. Back from the seaside, back from the beach.

But before that, there's the party, a gala more than three weeks in the making. Poor Inès, the governess who has been sent across the road, was in tears yesterday at the thought of missing the party. Asked to look after the elderly gentleman, she was busy making herbal tea in the stuffy, overheated room, and glancing out of the window from time to time. Inès could see the garden opposite, the path surrounded by gray lawns, a tiny corner of the bench concealed in the bushes, and the last little boy searching for his hoop. As soon as the elderly gentleman had gulped down his bowl of herbal tea, slipped on his spectacles and opened his big book, she sat down by the window. In the large gray garden, the tops of the old trees were trembling, and the young trees quivering all over. Further back was the tiny house, lit by a small light in its center. What were her two friends doing? Were they preparing for the party at least?

In the house opposite, in the dark night of the garden, the governesses are playing cards. Eléonore who seems so straitlaced is laughing like a madwoman.

Her cheeks are bright pink. She shakes out her wet hair and tosses her head back. One of the little boys has sat down in a large leather armchair and is leaning on his hoop as though on the rail of a ship's bridge. He watches the two governesses smoking sleek little cigarettes and playing cards. From time to time, he reaches down and spears an olive in a large china bowl next to the armchair, while holding the hoop steady with his other hand.

Another little boy is standing beneath the ponderously beating clock. Wearing knee breeches, his hands clasped behind his back, he's leaning forward slightly to make sure his feet are properly aligned within the floor squares. The right side of his face is concealed by a lock of stiff hair.

All through the house, on the stairs and landings, little boys march up and down, passing each other in silence. Sometimes a hoop trundles down the stairs and bounces across the wide hall. Only once does it pass through the hall without stopping and on into the salon, catching on a vase on one of the side tables. Whereupon children arrive six or seven at a time to pick up the pieces.

Were you to base an assessment of the governesses' professional skills on this particular evening, you would conclude that Monsieur and Madame Austeur had been most remiss in hiring the services of such a scatterbrained band of young women. You would even wager there was something fishy going on.

Still, it's only fair to say that, when it comes to throwing parties, the governesses are in a class of their own. In every other department of life—as far as one can judge from the time they've spent in the service of Monsieur and Madame Austeur—their imagination seems a little sluggish, as though held in check by a bizarre sense of propriety. But the moment a party or a birthday is involved—or any other commemorative event, for that matter—that same imagination, which a second before had been dead to the world, springs to life, opening its arms and shaking its legs about, and then, with an elegant thrust of the hips, diving into the thick of things.

In acknowledgement of their gift, Monsieur and Madame Austeur, who have done a fair bit of entertaining in their day, have appointed the governesses to a more senior position, albeit one that has yet to be properly defined: "mistresses of games and pleasures," say, or something along those lines. With their legendary generosity, they have thrown open the upstairs salons to the three young women so that they can install their offices and work spaces there, complete with paper lanterns, hoops, and background actors; "even acrobats, if need be," graciously added

Monsieur Austeur, marveling at their mastery of an art for which he himself, alas, had long since lost the knack.

Still, one may feel he had been unwise to entrust the governesses with the keys to the bedrooms and back rooms, the first-floor cupboards and dressing-table drawers, without consulting Madame before-hand. Having received no prior warning of their astonishing display, Madame was most put out. All day she roamed through the gardens in her long gray gown, pulling up flowers by their roots. That evening at dinner, however, after Monsieur Austeur had pla-cated her with a discreet caress between the hallway and the dining room, she was all smiles.

Today Monsieur and Madame Austeur are at the seaside. Tomorrow they'll come back with the little maids and one or two friends no doubt, in the long car the little boys are so taken with.

The festivities always begin in the same fashion. For the first few evenings, the governesses shut them-selves up in their rooms, where they have fits of the vapors and palpitations and break out in hives. On one occasion — though only once, it's true — their fainting fits occurred in the hallway and on the stairs. Monsieur Austeur came rushing over, then went to fetch smelling salts, while his wife Julie stood there,

clutching her pale arms at the sight of the governesses stretched out lifeless at her feet. Generally
speaking, however, things pass off more smoothly.
The governesses blush and flutter their eyelashes at
dinner, overturn a soup tureen, burst into tears, and
run up to their rooms. At this point Madame Austeur
starts humming a sentimental air and darting knowing glances at Monsieur Austeur. "It's high time they
were married, high time they were married," croons
Monsieur Austeur, wickedly. And the two spouses
exchange smiles like model parents over their daugh-
ters' first flushes of adolescence.

But let's follow the governesses more closely. After all, they're not sixteen anymore. And they don't
dream much as a rule. So what's all this playacting
about?

Eléonore and Laura are on excellent terms with Inès.
She has a gift for conversation, which they urge her
to cultivate, a way with words that "destines her for
great things," as they sweetly put it. From time to
time, when the elderly gentleman is taking a nap or
playing solitaire, the three of them stroll through the
garden together, arm in arm. Inès grumbles that she
never has a chance to practice her skills: the elderly
gentleman often falls silent, and the other household
staff are simply not up to par. Only in the company of

her friends can she broaden her knowledge, show off her conversational skills and polish her wit.

Next they discuss men. It's their favorite subject when they're practicing elocution. To hear them speak, you would think they had never set eyes on a man except through the garden gates. They describe the road the men take, and the little waves they give them. They add a few details, embroidering a bit if something significant is missing. They question each other. They compare the men with Monsieur Austeur, look for similarities and differences, and wind up, all three, at the end of the afternoon when the garden is growing cold, pressed up against the gates like dead butterflies.

They're not naive, however. Eléonore lived with Tom for six years, Laura has had seven love affairs and Inès a similar number.

All three are wearing yellow dresses as they stand pressed up against the garden gates at dusk. The road outside the gates has a speed bump, then a bend just after that, but it's not very practical for gauging faces. Ideally, the passersby need to be on foot. That way the governesses can see them coming and get a good look before they notice. By the time they stop at the gates with their hands in their pockets, the governesses know all kinds of things about them. Inès, for example, knows that this one isn't her type. Eléonore

tightens her belt, perches on her high heels and puffs
up her hair. Laura prepares a few questions.

From time to time, a car pulls up opposite these
three large butterflies and a man steps out. His meaning as he waves at them couldn't be more plain. He
rattles the gate and wants to come in. They stand
their ground. Sometimes he shouts because he
wants them, and then engages them in a terrifying
conversation. They reply, together or in turn, though
it's practically the same voice. Sometimes he cries,
so they offer him a bottom or a breast, a mouth, a
few hands. Since there are three of them, he rushes
off to get friends, other men. It's too good an opportunity to be missed. They come back in cars, ten or
fifteen men in all, and whole evenings go by in this
way: three yellow governesses pressed up against the
gates, and all these men milling around in the gray
twilight, in the countryside under the tall trees by the
speed bump and then the bend in the road.

That said, there's nothing venal or flighty, nothing
in the least bit unsavory, about the governesses. No
unfortunate rumor has ever tarnished their reputation. What unnerves them, it seems, is the excessive
silence of the households they wait upon. For though
it's conducive to reading, thinking and raising little
boys who are champion hoop rollers, and to the elderly gentleman's repose and the waning love of Mon-

sieur and Madame Austeur, there are times when the silence under the tall trees in the garden, in the salons and hallways, is so forbidding that it scares the governesses to be living there. And so they seek distractions.

They're allowed out, of course, but where can they go? They have no family or parents, and not much of a past either, which well and truly died the day they entered the service of Monsieur and Madame Austeur. On that day, they had to put everything behind them, and here is what happened: all the trees they had ever known—the ones in the school playground, for example, and the ones outside grandma's house and along the road to the beach—came rushing into Monsieur and Madame Austeur's garden, lining up side by side with the elms and the oaks, and then disappearing inside them. The same thing happened with houses, barns, châteaux, and whole towns. They all came storming through the wide-open gates the morning of the governesses' arrival, then on into the house, so that by the time the first night had fallen Monsieur and Madame Austeur's home had swallowed up a considerable quantity of roof beams, tiles, chimney stacks, and still-ticking grandfather clocks.

Eléonore had gone so far as to suggest that their new life seemed endowed with rather alarming powers. Laura, on the other hand, was delighted to have an entire universe at her fingertips, loved to unwind there, and for a long time would refuse to go out. Her days off would be spent exploring the garden, and even Inès—who pleaded with her repeatedly to come over for tea at the elderly gentleman's house— had to wait three months before receiving a visit.

Six in the evening. The sky's transparent and the garden's cold. The little boys have disbanded and are drifting around on the lawns. Some are seated in clusters of twos and threes, naked beneath their white shorts and pale-colored jumpers. The day has been arduous and joyful. From dawn to dusk they've been running around behind their hoops, screaming and jumping around in the tall grass. The governesses seemed out of their minds that day. They had just given the little boys a good scolding when, by a stroke of ill luck, a ball shattered the glass panes of the greenhouse. Thrusting her head out of her bedroom window, Eléonore glanced round and snapped at her pupils to go and find somewhere else to play. She seemed very busy, and her large brown head immediately vanished behind the net curtains. So they went into the greenhouse, which was normally off-limits, sat down for a moment among the mildewed terra-cotta pots, the hairy-leaved begonias and the gardening tools, and then stretched out under the flowers and told each other stories.

Arthur claims to have seen the governesses' un-dergarments. He was hiding in the bushes when they came along, their long yellow skirts passing over the flowers like candle snuffers. They were pressing their hands together excitedly and whispering. They stopped for a long time by the bushes where the little boy had been lying on his back, daydreaming. They shifted about: a few steps to the side, then back in his direction. Eléonore's dainty shoes were stained with mud. A corner of her skirt had caught on the brambles—she wasn't wearing stockings, and the tops of her legs were the color of buttercups.

Gregory roars with laughter at Arthur's tale. When it comes to girls, he says, he knows zillions of much funnier stories: the one, for example, about the two little girls who appeared at the garden gates last year. He got everything he wanted, it seems, they came by four times, four afternoons in a row, through the gap in the wall, they remained standing, it's true—they didn't want to lie down—but hitched up their blue dresses, moving their arms and legs up and down and turning round as he'd instructed them to do. The tall one was putting on airs, so he picked up a stick, at which point she started turning like the other one. It's like being at the circus, he says.

The older boy doesn't say anything. The night before, unable to sleep, he had stood at the window of his room, gazing out at the countryside for a long time before glancing over at the house opposite, at the far end of the garden. At the center of the house a window was lit. He could make out a motionless figure who, like him, was up late, examining the countryside. It didn't occur to him to wave at it. Was it a woman? A man? It was too far away to tell. There was something voluptuous about being alone in the expanse of gray lawns, with this other figure up late like him. You couldn't see the garden gates whose gildings had faded at dusk, leaving a huge gap like an empty stadium between the boy's window and the house opposite.

For the party, fifty vases, fifty chandeliers and the same number of lanterns are to be installed. They don't do things by halves around here. For a party, you need a dazzling array of splendors—the imagination in full flight, overflowing. Not that the governesses needed any reminding of this: on previous years they had clanged so many cymbals and banged so many drums that every man and woman for miles around, and even a few curious dogs, had come trotting over to gaze hungrily at the scene through the garden gates.

This year, the day of the party coincides with the return of Monsieur and Madame Austeur, so the merrymaking will be at its height. There'll be a journey in a hot-air balloon, a plane trip, and games in the river and the black garden under the enormous trees. In the house, the windows will remain lit from dusk to daybreak.

Everyone will rant and rave, dash along the paths and throw their hands up in despair while spinning around. They're allowed to bring sticks and thrash the air and the grass with a vengeance. They're allowed to unhitch the horses and gallop through the garden clinging to their necks, to tear through the foliage, then fall in a heap and lie there in the horses' hot breath. They're also allowed to dance naked, drink naked, and expose themselves all of a sudden on the front porch, flailing their arms and letting out hideous squeals that make everyone laugh.

In the meantime, the governesses are lacing the toddlers' sandals, smoothing the hair of the mop-heads, and holding their arms out to stroke the tear-stained cheeks of the boys who are frightened of the party. They have nothing to fear, they tell them, all they have to do is watch the others and do likewise, or stand there quietly on their own if that's what they prefer.

Eléonore seems so full of life that Gustave finds it scary. He doesn't dare take a close look at her. Inès is clacking her heels on the tiled floor, rat-a-tat-tat, rat-a-tat-tat, and swaying around. Laura is on the verge of suffocating as she tightens a soft braided lambskin belt around her slender waist. Rat-a-tat-tat, rat-a-tat-tat, the three of them dance and tap their feet.

All they're waiting for now is Monsieur and Madame Austeur, the long car and the little maids who will scurry around serving wine. The horses have been groomed, the hot-air balloon is spread out next to its basket on the lawn, and the musical instruments are lined up in a row in the hall.

The garden gates haven't stopped squeaking as they slowly open to let in delivery boys laden with platters of fish and jellied pheasant, bowls of cream, chilled wines, and the birds that will be released from the windows. Someone's hanging a last paper lantern above the porch, someone else is shimmying up a tree. Four or five little boys fling themselves from the ground-floor windows, rush up the steps and through the reception rooms, then start all over again.

Inès is trying out a riding crop. Raising her arm high in the air, she cracks it down with all her might against the floor. You don't know whether to be scared or to clap your hands in the presence of this sparkly eyed animal tamer—it's delightful. Everyone jumps back slightly and cries out: "Stop! Stop! You're crazy!" Eléonore has put a record on the gramophone player, and the booming music can be heard all the way up in the attic where the little boys who don't want to take part in the party are lying low.

The preparations are almost complete, but the car still doesn't arrive. They wait, tapping their feet. They don't want to spoil the party, so they're only pretending to play. Time and again, the little boys go into the garden to keep a lookout, poking their heads through the bars of the gates.

Everything's in place. The moment Monsieur and Madame Austeur come through the gates in their long black car, the party will begin. A trumpet will sound, and from every quarter grinning figures will appear, falling over one another and screaming and shouting just for the fun of it. The lawn will be seething with life, and in the car they'll split their sides laughing. Monsieur Austeur will say: "Aren't they clever! We were so right to hire them, don't you think, Madame Austeur?" And Madame Austeur will cock her little head and smile. The maids will want to get down and join the merry troupe, but won't dare ask. The elderly gentleman will have adjusted his telescope beforehand and won't miss a thing.

Dusk is setting in and the long car still hasn't arrived. The governesses are seated next to one another in the hall, on chairs lined up against the wall. The little boys are tired of jumping through windows, and, in any case, Eléonore has just forbidden it, giving the youngest of the toddlers a sharp slap. They're strolling around on the lawns now, laughing quietly to themselves.

Night falls. On the second floor weeping can be heard. The governesses have uncorked a bottle of wine and had a dish of fowl and a few walnuts brought for them, and are picking absentmindedly at their food with their fingers. In the distance the gate squeaks. They spring to their feet and, snatching up their cymbals, stand for a minute or two with pricked ears. A sound of car tires on the gravel? No. Nothing. They sit down again. A little boy comes over and asks permission to go to bed; others follow him up the staircase in silence. On the lawn, the hot-air balloon and its basket are no longer visible. The horses have stopped whinnying in their stalls.

A few more minutes go by like this, then an hour. In the house across the way, the elderly gentleman has packed up his telescope and retired for the night. Slowly, without exchanging a word, the governesses go up to their rooms, stay there for a while, then come back down. When they open the front door, you can see them for a moment in the light from the hall, standing on the porch. They're wearing yellow gowns and seem to be inspecting the night. Then they slip out onto the path and disappear under the trees.

THE GOLDEN GATES HAVE opened, letting a stranger in. Eléonore watches him closely, while Laura stands at an open window, holding her breath.

He makes his way across the lawns, stops to observe the branches of a tree, runs his hand over the bark, looks right, looks left, then walks on ahead. They can't make out his face for the moment. He walks slowly, throwing his head back from time to time, as though filling his lungs with the cold, damp air. In the house, the governesses have assembled and are asking themselves: "Who is he? Where is he from? Should we let him in?"

Instead of walking toward the house, he veers off suddenly and disappears beneath the trees. With a clack of wings, a bird flies up from a thicket. Eléonore and Laura rush downstairs and appear on the porch, out of breath, their hair a bit disheveled. They're not going to let him vanish like that. He has walked into the trap of their vast, lunar privacy; they get their nets out, they're going to capture him and keep him there. In their blue and brown dresses, they stride off into the woods in pursuit, parting the undergrowth with their razor-sharp ankle boots. He can't be far. Over there is a patch of green darting between the leaves. It's him. The hunt begins.

Is he scared? You'd think he was being pursued by two wild animals. Is that him running now? Yes, there he is, breaking into a brisk trot, bounding across the meadow. They know all the short cuts. There's no harm in waiting, they tell themselves—*take your time*.

And their skirts catch on the brambles, tearing in places. Rainwater from the high bracken splashes onto their trim, polished shoes.

Their bare arms are covered with scratches, their legs streaked with rainwater, their skirts filled with odors.

It's not every day you get to hunt in a household like this. There's no quarry most of the time. This one will be tackled head-on, licked, bitten and devoured in a ladylike manner. And once he's exhausted and has nothing further to offer, they'll leave him. He'll lie there like a babe in arms, naked on the sage-green meadow, while they will have something to reminisce about on those interminable winter evenings when you stand at the window, longing desperately for a stranger to arrive.

They make their way down a narrow lane hollowed out like a ditch between two low dry stone walls. All you can see for a second is the tops of their skulls and their hair flying level with the meadow. They can hear him now. He's there, panting, gasping for breath as he crashes around; he's more or less stopped crashing, in fact. He's going to surrender. He can't take it anymore. Eléonore has pounced on him, seizing him from behind with both hands. They've laid him out on the ground and are unbuttoning his trousers. He's very handsome, a bit soiled by the mud and rain, but that only makes him more desirable. Laura has unlaced the strings of his drawers with her teeth. The breasts of one of the young women have slipped out of her blouse, the other woman has already hitched the skirt of her dress up around her waist. They're going to settle his hash; and settle their own affairs while they're at it.

Growing gentle again in the midst of their frenzy, they pull out a terrified sex. Eléonore has taken it in hand and is squeezing it, gripping it with her fingers and sliding it slowly, very slowly, up and down. Laura has hitched up her brown skirt and is seated on the stranger's face. His eyelids have closed, but he's breathing heavily and fast. Little by little, his pale member reddens and starts to rise. He breathes in the scent of Laura the way he breathed in the smell of the air and the wet trees a moment ago. He no longer feels scared.

His member is erect now, the plum-violet glans shining between Eléonore's slender fingers. Pulling up her blue skirt, she squats down on top of it, gently impaling herself on the hot, hard, smooth, erect thing sinking inside her.

It's six in the evening by the time they've finished. The man has been bled dry, his handsome, open hands lying lifeless beside his body. Because he's cold and doesn't move, they put his clothes back on. Then, a bit the worse for wear, but happy and replete, they make their way back to the house in silence.

They walk through the woods entwined in each other's arms, their lips bruised and swollen, their bodies appeased at last. In the garden, the children have come out to play. They surround the governesses, cheering them on like victors returning from war. The boys dance all the way to the porch, then disappear with them into the wide, freezing corridor.

Tonight, Inès will come over. They'll play solitaire and talk about men. And tomorrow, or in a month, or a year—who knows?—the golden gates will open suddenly, as if by magic, and another stranger will succumb to their spell, trapped in the warm night of their private world.

DUST ON THE HILLS in this month of July. The air is so hot, the sun so fiery, that the grass is scorched, yellow and dry. They've taken the children for a walk. Lying down, their flesh pricked by twigs, they watch little wisps of cloud being shunted across the azure sky. A face forms, then the mouth widens, the nose juts out, the hair grows matted: it's an animal now, waiting to pounce, then melting away in midleap. The little boys are playing, and their cries are like the cries you hear in dreams. The real world, meanwhile, is hot, hard and sizzling, buzzing with insects.

The governesses lie on their backs smoking little cigarettes, then blowing out the light smoke and filling their lungs with air. They've pulled their skirts up over the tops of their thighs so that they can feel

the sun on their bare legs, unbuttoned their blouses
so that it can flow between their breasts.

In the distance they can hear a solitary cowbell tin-
kling, then a dog bark that seems to come from a cave
somewhere. The sun burns their skin, tiny runnels of
water trickle down their necks and armpits and the
folds of their groins onto their sleepy flesh. On their
hair spread out across the grass, airy dragonflies walk
as if on water.

Their minds drift back to the stranger: his ema-
ciated face when they had drained all the sap and
drawn all the honey from him; his ardent, blind
hands searching for something to grasp; his erect
member which seemed not to belong to him anymore. They'd love to find him again, restore him to
his former state, then dip back into him and draw
out that sense of bliss without which they feel bereft.
Eléonore has sat up, her face crimson, dazed by the
heat. Laura is indolently wiping her streaming body
with the folds of her skirt. Dark-haired Inès has fallen
asleep in her red dress.

The children have wandered off and there's no one
around. They pull off their underpants, toss their sandals, skirts and blouses behind them, then, stretching
out naked next to their friend, whose red skirt is billow-
ing slightly in the breeze, surrender to the dragonflies
who have begun their assault on their gleaming fleeces.

Eléonore's is a bulge between two white thighs that will later turn pink in the sun. Curly and less matted, Laura's is like a patch of lichen below the sweet-smelling belly.

The sun nestles between their thighs, warming the closed slit gorged with memories and expectation. It's as though he was there, the stranger, coming toward them. He doesn't have a name. They couldn't care less where he comes from, they have no intention of marrying him. All they want is for him to comfort these bodies inconsolable at being cut off from him. To placate the storm in their bellies with his delicious hands, his delicious mouth, his delicious sex.

Of course, he'll have to go at it again and again, once, twice, ten times perhaps, for it takes a while for a storm to subside. It's as though, rumbling around inside that storm, there was thunder from millions of years ago, the lightning of yesteryear and the lightning of today. To extinguish all those fires lit so many times all those eons ago he'll have to keep pounding at them, over and over; and since in placating those ancestral storms he'll have whipped up new ones, there'll be no end to his labor.

They'll love him, yes, but only while he's inside them. The moment he's outside, they'll hate him. They'll pretend to love him, to make sure he comes back, but behind their sweet nothings and tender glances will be two frenzied nymphs who will tear him to pieces if he doesn't hurry up.

For the stranger, being tucked up in their silky soft cocoons is a homecoming. He could happily sleep there forever. If he's tired, it's because he's walked a long way and worked hard. What he would like to do is relax for a while and be welcomed into their nest. He wants to lie down inside them and stare at the sky, listen to the sea. But when he does lie down in them, he's tormented; he'll never find rest there.

At first, they didn't know how to placate these storms. Time and experience are needed. At first, they thought you had to rush everywhere, so they'd race around the garden like madwomen, climbing trees, scaring the birds away, stamping their feet at the gates, hurling all kinds of objects at each other. They would swim or read—feverishly, all night— devour an entire pheasant, tear their dresses, kiss the maids. Then came the first stranger, whom they didn't trust one little bit. They had heard about love, they had heard about men and the power they wielded. It filled them with dread. They would hide behind the curtains in their rooms, or in some dark corner in a corridor, behind a doorway, and from there would study him.

If he approached, their faces would be inscrutable, their bodies dumb. They didn't really have bodies, in fact. So long as the stranger remained outside them, they could examine him all they liked, they still didn't know a thing about him. And it was because of this fiercely guarded secret that they eventually went up to him.

They emerged from the shadows where you can see without being seen and walked into the center of the lighted room. They looked him straight in the eye. When there was desire in his gaze they knew that it was somewhere nearby that the secret was hidden. So they tried to open the door, but only a little, just to get a glimpse inside. Of themselves they gave nothing away—not a thing, not even a fingertip. They wanted to know the secret, but without having to share it with him. Again they failed. When they opened the door slightly, they saw the same thing they had seen in his gaze. Nothing more than that. The secret was still further back. They would have to go up to him and let him touch them. They gave him a mouth, a breast, occasionally an entire body, but even when he was inside them, it wasn't enough. They were still in the dark because they didn't feel a thing.

Then, one day, something in their body stirred. Something that went coursing through their limbs, igniting a million sparks that began to glow day and night. They stopped being afraid, opened their golden gates, and sat quietly without moving, waiting for him to walk into the silky trap that was the secret of his own desire.

They came to know quite a few strangers. A surprising number, in fact, for three governesses locked up in the dark night of a garden. Living as they did, they could easily have never met a soul. But either the stranger would lose his way in the garden, or else, coming in out of curiosity, he would take a step too far, and, with a little click, the golden gates would close behind him.

They loved watching a stranger arrive. There were times, in fact, when they liked that more than anything, for as long as he advanced, ignorant yet dimly aware of a summons that was never clearly formulated as such, they were all-powerful. Once he had been bound hand and foot and consumed, on the other hand, they turned back into three poor little governesses. If it hadn't been for the understanding between them, they would have taken their own lives in despair perhaps, since the moment the man had been conquered, they would return to the boundless void of their present home. They had memories, of course; but since when are memories enough to make three distraught governesses happy?

For not once—and this is not the least interesting part of their story—did they invite a stranger to stay. Apparently, it never crossed their mind. A stranger in the house? Good God, no! In the garden: fine. Standing, seated, supine, devouring, devoured: fine. But coming through the door into the great, silent house? No, under no circumstances.

Why though? Was there a treasure hidden in one of the rooms, so that they had to forbid anyone from entering it? There was nothing of the kind. There were a few valuable objects, of course, and a handful of little boys, it's true—but since when has anything of that sort prevented a lovestruck governess from inviting whomever she pleases?

There's the back room, of course, where Monsieur Austeur presides. It might well be him, the spoilsport standing in the governesses' way. There's also Madame Austeur and the little maids, but they're no great shakes. The figure they cut is insignificant. No, the obstacle is Monsieur Austeur. Not that he ever objects to anything; it's simply that his presence possesses strange virtues, which seep into and fill every nook and cranny of the house. It's as though, with Monsieur Austeur around, there was no room in the house for another male presence.

You can guess what happened next. In order to

devour their strangers at leisure, the governesses are inevitably going to think, sooner or later, of ridding themselves of Monsieur Austeur.

MONSIEUR AUSTEUR IS SEATED in his smoking room, puffing on his silky long cigars. Monsieur Austeur is the master of the house. It's midnight and everyone is asleep. At the heart of the house, he sits up late. The throbbing of the sleeping house travels out from him, and to him it returns. The signals he emits are slow and steady; those he receives back— from the governesses and Madame Austeur, who's tossing and turning on her pillow, from the little boys sleeping like logs and the young maids yawning and thinking about their sweethearts—stream in, brief and chaotic, from every corner of the house.

Ensconced in his armchair at the center of the room, he receives all these cries, these chirrups and yelps from the women and children of the house, and, shuffling them together in his heart, sends them back transformed, slow and steady like the signals from a lighthouse. Once he has done this, the governesses settle down in their beds, Madame Austeur falls asleep at last, the little boys begin dreaming, and the young maids can rest easy with a smile.

Monsieur Austeur's task is not a simple one. He's obliged to sit up late to keep order in the house: otherwise, danger threatens—the walls would crumble and the windows fly open with a bang. If he wasn't there watching over the heart of the house like a grandfather clock, who knows what would happen. The governesses would appear out of nowhere in their yellow dresses, panting for breath, the maids would start howling, the little boys would fling themselves out of the windows, and the ever so respectable Madame Austeur would rip open her gray dress and expose her skinny body naked on the porch, laughing like a madwoman, a wicked witch.

So he has to be there at night, regulating the breathing of the household with his heart, and, with his solitude held firmly in place by his large square armchair, counterbalancing the chaos that streams in from the bedrooms, prowls on the landings, pokes its nose out from under the doors.

When they hired the governesses the house had been peaceful. A bit too peaceful, perhaps. In those days, he didn't sit up late, for there was no need to.

At night, he would climb into the straitjacket of his square white bed and, in a kind of rage, try to get some sleep. He felt fretful, but didn't know why. He would press against his wife's pale body, derive little comfort from it and, in spite of the love he gave Madame Austeur, would feel his manhood unused.

It was chaos he needed. He was there to govern opposing forces, to conjure up sweet sounds and muffle shrill ones, to lead the orchestra with his baton, to blow on the embers and put out fires, to dispel darkness and raise the sun. Instead, here he was with a Madame Austeur who'd become an open book to him, obedient to his dreams, leaving him with nothing further to desire.

The day the governesses walked into the garden, Monsieur Austeur was standing behind the net curtains in the salon, keeping an eye out for their arrival. They advanced in single file: first Inès in a red dress, weighed down with hat boxes and bags, then Laura in a blue skirt, and, bringing up the rear, Eléonore, who was waving a long riding crop over the heads of a gaggle of little boys. He was amazed: it was life itself advancing. He rubbed his hands together and began jumping up and down in the salon. Into the garden they came, and with them a whole bundle of memories and desires, a throng of unfamiliar faces clutching at their dreams, their future children, their future sweethearts, the interminable cohort of their ancestors, the books they had read, the scents of flowers they had smelled, their blond legs and ankle boots, their gleaming teeth.

By noon, Monsieur Austeur had turned back into a man, and the house once more had a center—wherever Monsieur Austeur happened to be located. Each time he visited the greenhouse, strolled through the garden or went to inspect the orchard, the center of the house was there, standing meekly at his side. From the greenhouse or the garden path or the orchard he would share out, generously and fairly, the steady beatings of his heart. Around him concentric circles would form, radiating out to the far edges of his life. That's what living was.

For the governesses, moving in with Monsieur and Madame Austeur was like a homecoming. Whenever they lost their way in their new garden, all they had to do was climb into a tree and look for the smoke from Monsieur Austeur's cigar: as soon as they saw it drifting gently between the leaves they knew exactly where they stood in the maze of their new life.

Where were they from? It's hard to say. But it's safe to assume that, in spite of their young age, they had experienced some sort of tragedy in their life, at least one. What leads one to believe this is their eccentricity: too much joy, too much grief, too much appetite, too much silence, a strange frenzy. It's obvious there's a secret in their past. Nothing out of the ordinary perhaps, but something that has molded their character and shaped the way they move, the sound of their voices, their dreams, their habit of roaming around the garden with their hands pressed to their temples. The presence of that secret somewhere between the heart and the womb could also be said to have deprived them of free will, but then who can be said to possess free will? The governesses are like those clockwork toys that start walking when you wind a key in their back. Each morning, a key turns in their slim, aristocratic backs, and away they go, clapping their hands, rolling hoops, devouring strangers, spinning round, three little turns, each faster than the last. Every evening, they come home tired and a little more gentle. It's at times like these that you can talk to them and be heard. For a few hours, the machinery has wound down. At times like these they don't understand a thing about their gargantuan appetite. It horrifies and shames them. At times like these, they dream of being someone else and think it possible. They'd just need to jump around less, wear pale dresses perhaps, and change hairstyles. They vow to imitate Madame Austeur, to go out with her tomorrow gossiping about womanish things as they saunter past the clipped rosebushes, gathering up the wilted petals. Yet when tomorrow comes, they leap out of bed with a wicked gleam in their eye, grab their red dresses, break a window, lash out at the maids, run over to the gates, race across the lawns, sense an unfamiliar form hiding behind a dark tree, go over and start to pursue him, get dirty and tear their clothes.

Keeping a close watch on all this unruliness is Monsieur Austeur. He no more knows what he's doing than the governesses do, but he reins them in, so that everything is once more orderly, composed.

Every once in a while, they pretend to leave. Just to stir up the household, which, in spite of the governesses' outlandish behavior, is almost Apollonian in its staidness. It's also an opportunity to see Madame Austeur cry and Monsieur Austeur looking bewildered, which excites them no end.

Whenever they pretend to leave, they play their parts so well that everyone is taken in by their little game, including themselves. Even though they've played it a dozen times before, each time the result exceeds everyone's expectations: maximum distress, weeping and wailing, shamefaced confessions, shudders, a clean sweep of the past.

They begin by packing their bags with gritted teeth. Tipped off by the maids, Madame Austeur rushes upstairs, a handkerchief clutched to her trembling mouth. The governesses don't look up. With a bashful air, wringing her hands, Madame Austeur asks them the reason for this headlong departure. They turn icy gazes on her. Their despair is patent.

Carrying hatboxes and bags and wrapped in their traveling cloaks, they descend the stairs, always in single file, their minds made up. Monsieur Austeur comes out of the smoking room and tries to intervene. They march straight past him and arrive at the front door. He flings himself in the way, blocking their path. Without a word, they push past him onto the porch. He rushes down the steps and again blocks their way, pleading with outstretched arms. Again they push past him. He then jogs along behind them as they stride on ahead, their outraged faces staring up at the sky, the flesh of the iris inflamed, legs steady, backs arched. A horde of dismayed little boys has gathered round and accompanies them.

When the gates are in sight they slow their pace. It's barely noticeable, but the moment they do so Monsieur Austeur straightens up and heaves a discreet sigh of relief. They're strutting around now, swinging their hips, chatting among themselves, and shaking out their hair. They sit down by the edge of the path; they need "a little breather," they say. The fact that they're speaking means that the worst is over. Monsieur Austeur draws himself up to his full height, smooths his hair, straightens his jacket and casts an eye around the gardens. Back in the house, just visible behind the net curtains, Madame Austeur has sat down at last. The elderly gentleman has put down his telescope and is rubbing his hands, laughing quietly to himself.

They don't surrender their ground just yet. Instead, they wander nonchalantly over to the gates and poke their heads between the bars. Monsieur Austeur observes their every movement. The little boys have gathered round him in a semicircle. The governesses take a step forward, then a step to the side. Then, as though propelled by some mysterious resolve, they wheel round, push their way through the crowd, and march back up the path. The danger has passed. For the next week or so, they'll be treated like queens. Their every whim will be catered to. At a glance from one of them, Madame Austeur will rush upstairs to fetch something or Monsieur Austeur go out in the rain to look for a hoop that's gone missing. The little boys will know all their lessons by heart. The young maids will pin photos of the governesses above their beds.

And at night, when they go into the garden, the eyes trained on them from behind the windows and the glint from the telescope following them into the brushwood will give them the feeling they're cherished and loved and no longer alone in the world, and that in this huge dark garden with its enormous trees, they're protected, even when they're lost in the darkest undergrowth.

NOT EVERY STRANGER THEY meet is devoured in an afternoon. They also have genuine love affairs, relationships that endure, with a beginning, a climax and the inevitable downfall.

Their love life begins with a nondescript stranger whom they devour in an orderly fashion on a summer's afternoon. The moment they're back at the house, however, they want to see him again. Initially, this requires no great effort on their part, since the stranger is smitten and soon finds his own way there. He prowls beneath the windows, disturbs Monsieur Austeur's midnight vigils, clambers up the tangled branches of the Virginia creeper, and pops up on the governesses' balcony. Marvelous midnight revels ensue that they would never admit being so partial to. But, little by little, they're overcome with lust. It's no longer enough that he turns up at night, they want him there in the daytime, too. They want him all to themselves. They want him with no past and no other life than the love they feel for him.

It's at this point that the pangs of suffering sink into their tender flesh for the first time. They ignore them—they're not unpleasant, in fact. The stranger grows ten inches, his hair turns a deeper gold, his flesh tastier, his voice more resonant. They succumb.

In love they cease to possess that marvelous self-assurance that sent them striding through garden, woods and fields, lashing the wayside grass. They mellow. They mellow so much, in fact, that you'd think they were melting. Monsieur and Madame Austeur hardly recognize them, let alone the stranger. He preferred them high-handed and aloof, yet here they are welcoming him in a nightdress, shivering on the balcony, cooing and sighing. He hates having the upper hand and tries to restore them to their former state. He slips into their ardent bodies—but no, they want to purr like kittens, rub against him, be the under-dog. So the stranger, who had been so pliant up until now, swells out his chest, doesn't come by for four days, licks his chops, grabs them from behind, and wants to resume his journey. He leaves them in the lurch. They're not ashamed to beg. Or rather, they *are* ashamed, but beg just the same: "Sink your teeth into us, drag us by the hair all the way across the lawns, all the way up to the gates. And there, open us up, open the gates of the world for us, take us away, drag us out of this cage of silence where all we see is the sky."

They've started dreaming about his native countryside. They ask him to describe it, but he's at a loss for words. "Well . . . ," he says, "there are trees outside the house . . . and behind the house there's a railroad station." And so they begin dreaming, dreaming nonstop. One morning the station is pink and white, like a child's toy, a lovely little station with gleaming rails and the train that devoured Anna Karenina, with snow and a stationmaster. In the evening, it's a ramshackle old station, high up in the Alps, against a backdrop of dark mountains, with freight trains loaded with pine trunks. The next day, it's a busy station in a big city, with passengers bustling back and forth and trains screaming at each other like madmen. The governesses are scared, clapping their hands in excitement as their skirts flap around in the blast from the packed express trains screeching by. Outside the station are hotels with faded signs and tired red-plush reception areas, faux-bois doors and melancholy washstands. But all that's outside, and outside is a marked improvement on the ideal, radiant, frozen cage of their current abode. When the stranger mentions the tree outside his house, they concoct gardens with a handful of pebbles, imagine gardens choked with weeds and roads dappled with the shadows of leaves and sunlight.

Oh, if only they could leave! Run off with this man who has happened along, using him to pass through the gates and loving him because he can take them to a place where their bonds will be ever so gently loosened at last. So that, one day, each of them will be able to live and speak in her own name, love in her own name, be alone in the world, and free of the others at last.

Inès can take the road to the right, Laura the road to the left and Eléonore the one in the middle. Their paths will never cross again. Never. On the contrary, each of them will have a life of her own. But the stranger doesn't take them away. He refuses to drag them by the hair or drive them on before him. So they remain there, alone, burdened with their imaginary lives and imaginary homes, their imaginary children and imaginary conversations, and when you run into them they're not easy to understand because they're carrying around an invisible world which they draw on whenever they search for a word or a gesture or try to remember something. In that invisible world, they've spent ten years living with Tom, had two or three children and a home of their own. In that invisible world, they've lived to the age of forty, fifty, even eighty perhaps. Each of the governesses is composed of a bundle of memories blown up like a huge, shiny balloon . . . and, in another part of her, of a few rather pretty dresses, a pair of ankle boots, a riding crop, a house that doesn't belong to her, and a few combs, no doubt. As for their activities, they can be summed up as follows: keeping an eye on the little boys, racing around the garden like madwomen, devouring jellied pheasant and a few strangers along the way, and clapping their hands. And, as often as not, sinking into a silence and inertia that bode no good.

FOR A LONG TIME now, the elderly gentleman
has been watching them through his telescope. Each
day he notes down his observations. For example:
"Monday: Governesses in red dresses, stretched out
on the garden lawns all morning. Noon: Governesses
gone. Laura's head at bedroom window; Eléonore's
(bare) leg on porch. Afternoon: Governesses in
the woods. Eléonore squatting in an obscene—but
not disgraceful—manner on outstretched man.
Evening: Governesses seated on front porch steps,
smoking. Ardent faces. Night: If only I had a telescope that could see through net curtains!"

If you wanted to know about the governesses'
lives, he would be the one to ask. It's as though, with
the onset of old age and the infirmities that come
with it, he had decided to devote himself exclusively

47

to the governesses across the way. They know this and enjoy it. Alone in the dark night of their garden, how could they fail to enjoy being seen by at least one eye? It comforts them in a way. They're not literally alone in the house, of course, since there are also Monsieur and Madame Austeur, the little maids, and the little boys. But none of the latter is sufficiently detached from the governesses to actually see them live. They're part of their life, which is probably why the governesses are so afraid to leave. They would step through the gates, and all of a sudden the house would vanish, the garden would roll up like a rug, and the gates would collapse. They would look round and everything that had made up their past, their entire life up to that point, would have vanished. What keeps them there is that all of them have the impression — separately, in secret — of underwriting its reality. Were one of them to go missing, everything would disappear....

This, too, the elderly gentleman has jotted down in his notebook, for he doesn't simply describe things, he draws conclusions, makes suppositions, mulls things over, double-checks. He has never really sought to communicate with the neighbors across the way, for it would interfere with his observations. When he does address one of them, it's to remind himself what their voice sounds like, recall the skin tone of their delectable flesh, the click of their ankle boots with their shiny little heels. Once he has refreshed his memory, he abandons them to their fate and settles down for days on end at the window, his eye pressed to his telescope.

Sometimes they signal to him, and in a none too friendly manner. When Laura's pink cheeks and irresistible gaze appear in miniature at the other end of his telescope, all of a sudden he'll see her staring back at him, opening her mouth to point a snakelike tongue at him. Offended, and at the same time aroused, he looks away. Then he holds up his telescope again. All three are now framed in the disk of his lens, as though posing for a photograph. Eléonore plays the bride, clasping her hands and gazing ecstatically up to heaven. Laura plays the bridesmaid, plucking at the train of her sister's gown. Inès plays the bridegroom, gazing at her spouse with a look of ardent desire. Thrilled, he puts down his telescope for a second, then holds it up again. They're naked now and playing The Three Graces. Eléonore and Laura, who have their hair up and their faces in profile, are baring their pale, chubby bottoms to him. Inès, meanwhile, is standing full face, one hand placed absentmindedly over her barely concealed thatch, and staring into space. At times, they're frankly obscene, and the elderly gentleman, though very distinguished, revels in it, as when the two Graces with their backs to the window bend forward all of a sudden and part their buttocks for the figure observing them, wriggling the great white smiling moons of their behinds at him. At the same moment, the one in the middle clutches feverishly at her breasts while pointing her dark crotch at the telescope. The elderly gentleman is sweating. Then they're tired of playing around. They gather up their dresses, chat for a moment, and, without so much as a glance at the figure observing them, dash up the steps of the porch and disappear into the hall.

Monsieur and Madame Austeur have also seen them—she from behind net curtains, he from the window of his study. They didn't get the same thrill out of it as the elderly gentleman and are lost in thought. Madame Austeur has no idea why the governesses act in this way, but senses that the last thing she should do is to try to put a stop to their little games or prevent them from happening again in the future. Monsieur Austeur is equally in the dark. It all takes place in a world he's no longer part of. It's as though he had seen the governesses dreaming.

The elderly gentleman has folded up his telescope. That's enough for today, he can put aside his spyglass and settle down for the night. He has seen the "holy of holies," he tells himself, and, his wishes fulfilled, falls blissfully asleep. As for the governesses, they've forgotten about their little performance already. They go up to their rooms as innocently as they had come down, with the feeling of having earned a good night's rest. When they fall asleep in their beds, the full moon is shining above the garden, radiant and still. They dream. In Laura's dream, a large, royal blue door opens onto an unfamiliar stretch of countryside. She leaps out of a fireplace surrounded by crackling yellow and orange flames, walks over to the blue door and opens it.

SO WHERE ARE THEY off to this morning? From the way they're dressed, it looks as if they're going to a party. Is someone getting married perhaps? Celebrating a first communion? Are the neighbors holding a reception? They're decked out in their finest silk-lined capes, their brightly polished ankle boots, and their various dresses: red for Eléonore, blue for Laura, meadow-green for Inès.

Not enough has been said about the governesses' beauty. They're irresistible. The noblest of the three is Eléonore. The carriage of her head, her smooth auburn hair, which she wears in a chignon, and her Grecian profile with its pronounced, pale nostrils, conjure up a woman in an Ingres painting. Then life breaks out, a blush appears, the locks of her hair fall loose, her body rounds graciously out, and you have one of Boucher's brazen hussies, the buttocks now pale and majestic, now mocking and well-rounded, with little dimples everywhere.

More gentle and tenderhearted, Laura is the most sensual in the way she moves around. As for Inès, she's without question the liveliest of the three, pliant as the stem of a flower and very Spanish with her dark eyes and her ebony-black hair coiled like a snake around the ravishing curves of her skull.

When they change dresses, a multitude of different women appear, depending on the color they're wearing. Eléonore is in her element in red: it's the Eléonore we're all familiar with, aristocratic and resolute. In blue, she's a thousand times more romantic. In blue, she would never risk baring her behind to the elderly gentleman across the way. In blue, she strolls up and down the garden paths, lost in thought, as we saw her on the first page—a true governess, a tutor almost, perhaps even a widow. In green, she harbors venomous thoughts and has a wicked gleam in her eye. In a green dress she's quite capable of devouring a stranger—joylessly, ardently—or exposing her icy behind to whoever wishes to see it.

Red has a soothing influence on Inès, who's on fire the moment she's naked. Gentler than her, it burns at a lower level of intensity than her flesh. In blue she's unforgettable. It suits her so well, in fact, that a stranger passing by that day couldn't fail to fall madly in love with her.

Laura in blue is invisible. In green, she's stunning. But only in red can she give herself up to a stranger. On her pale, dreamy flesh, red appears like the revelation of her inmost self.

When all three are wearing yellow, anything can happen. It's the wild color, the color that frees them, the color in which they feel naked and exposed, spellbound. You only see them in yellow at the gates, at night, or on days when they run amok in a blind fury. Yellow turns them into heartless, spiteful wretches. On days like that, they're armed with stilettos, nurture an asp between their breasts, and cut through the tall grass like the Queen of Hearts slicing off the heads of her gardeners. Many a male has kicked himself for meeting them on a day like that. Slender and razor-sharp, they walked all over him, cutting short any desire with their teeth, then leaving him there, panting for breath, on the meadow.

This morning, however, they're like swallows. Let's follow them, leaping along like a young monkey, swinging from branch to branch above their heads. As they make their way up the path, the trees grow taller, the path opens out, the earth grows brighter. They're on their way to a wedding.

There's no need to leave the grounds to reach the

neighbors' house. An opening in the woods leads straight into their garden, where four red and white striped tents have been installed, with little streamers fluttering in the wind. A good hundred guests are milling around on the lawn, including at least two women who look like parakeets. There are also a number of young women drifting around who offer the governesses serious competition. Slim young women with glossy black hair, all kinds of women, in fact, leading the governesses to fear they are no longer alone in the world. As a result, they become tongue-tied and a little stiff, a hundred times less fetching than in the enchanted realm of the Austeurs' garden.

When Monsieur and Madame Austeur are in view, things are different. The governesses shine in their presence, and no one but the governesses could please them to quite the same degree. They have no difficulty twisting the Austeurs round their little finger, attaching the bait that will leave them open-mouthed, then yanking it out while they lie there gasping for breath, their tongues torn out. It's become a game, in fact, one they all love to play. But today, at the neighbors' wedding party, they're on their own. And since we have described them looking their best, we must now describe them, without mincing our words, looking their worst.

Stiff and pinched, Eléonore is standing like a wall-flower in a corner of one of the tents. Laura is in a sweat; the swallow has turned into a drab, stammering, gauche young girl. Yes, it really is that bad. Inès is too proud ever to lose her beauty, but here she is in the middle of the lawn, a glass of champagne in her hand, straight as a knife, slim as a rope, and though she's doing her best to be sociable, her hawkish eye is roving over the throng of guests. The neighbors chat and joke politely with all three, but the governesses are hard pressed to find the simplest, most innocent words in reply. The sounds that knock against their palates, the words that come out of their mouths astonish them—words and intonations they didn't know they possessed, images they're not familiar with, remarks that don't belong to them. They try to stop the words from coming out, to turn them into something different the moment they form, but to no avail. Powerless and not a little humiliated, they're present at their own downfall.

They're no longer young swallows winging their way home but poor, crestfallen young women who don't dare look one another in the eye. They go up to their rooms in silence. And who, I ask you, on such an evening, would be so heartless as to follow them?

THE LITTLE BOYS OCCUPY a great deal of the governesses' time. After all, they were hired to look after the boys and drum a few notions into them. They love playing at schoolmistresses, watching the little boys line up in pairs at the ring of the bell, then taking them off on a walk where they'll gather chestnuts and plane leaves for their plant collections.

When the little boys go walking in the forest, they long to lose their way, leading the governesses off through undergrowth and thicket, meadow and marsh, eager to give themselves a good scare—and no doubt to come to the governesses' rescue as well. They begin by gathering leaves for their collections: soft round poplar leaves, wafer-thin like the host at communion; the inevitable plane leaves; and horse chestnut leaves, which they pull apart until all that remains is a skeleton like that of a prehistoric fish.

Laden with pebbles, leaves, and flowers whose heads are already drooping, they sit themselves down in a meadow for lunch. The governesses let out a yawn and lower their guard. They unlace their boots. They even strip naked sometimes, and the little boys gaze at them in silence, petrified. For the rest of their lives, they will love only governesses naked in a soft green meadow, their long thighs in the grass, the gleaming thatch of hair where pale yellow butterflies alight, their tender, dreamy breasts.

Some of them are allowed to sketch the governesses. And beneath their sketches they write, in capital letters: THE THREE GRACES. The older ones timidly reach out a hand. They're allowed to cup a breast, run their hand along the contour of a thigh, hover above the thatch of hair. But not more than that. Then it's time for dancing, a moment the boys adore. The governesses rise to their feet and, to the sound of tambourines and pipes, start to dance, lifting a long leg in time to the beat, then an arm, then another leg and another arm. The older boys lie in the grass, watching them, happy as kings. The dance goes on for a long time. It can even last until nightfall. They've forgotten about their chestnuts and plant collections, the buckeyes in their prickly casings, the bluebells and bindweed. They've lit a fire and are clapping their hands. Animals appear on the edge of the woods, like a scene in a fairy tale. You can see their dark forms moving around behind the trees and hear the soft stamp of their delicate hooves: a hundred eyes, some bright, some dark, some black, some red, stare out at the governesses as they dance on the meadow, licked by the flames that leap back and forth to the beat of the tambourines.

Then all of a sudden they've had enough, feel frozen by the cold night air, stop dancing, and put their clothes back on. It's time to go home. They tramp through the forest together, silent and at one, their step more harmonious than when they first set out. It's not cold anymore, their bags no longer feel heavy. They've just shared a secret that will nourish them in the dead hours of winter, inject a zestful new sap into the dry trunks of the tall black trees, and install a fiery young spring beneath the ice. Henceforth, the little boys will know that life is there, shaking its tambourine, and that all you need to do is press your ear to the ground to feel it beating and claim your due.

FOR SOME TIME NOW, Madame Austeur has been thinking of marrying off the governesses. It's nothing new. More than once she has broached the subject with Monsieur Austeur, discussing it with him for many a long hour in the salon.

Monsieur Austeur has nothing against the idea, which he thinks perfectly sensible, but he can hardly be said to be throwing his full weight behind it. While Madame Austeur gabbles on, he nods his head, as if in agreement—and, should the governesses happen to be walking by at that moment, "Well, well," they say, from the other side of the window, "they're discussing our marriage." Not that this keeps them from continuing to nibble on the thin, hairy stem of a poppy, idle as they always are when something is afoot. At the sound of their steps on the gravel drive,

Madame Austeur lowers her voice and Monsieur Austeur looks slightly embarrassed. "There's no mad rush ...," he says to put a stop to their conversation.

But Madame Austeur is not one to admit defeat. Going up to her bedroom, she pulls out her notebook, grabs a pencil, and starts drawing up a list of suitors. This one, for example, has a bad reputation, but then people are starting to gossip about the governesses, too. Perhaps he'd be suitable for Eléonore, on the face of it the fieriest of the three? Mind you, there's Laura too.... For Laura, there's a neighbor who would fit the bill, if only she were a little more ... modest. More self-effacing. Laura would be perfect if only she were willing to keep up a proper conversation with a stranger instead of breaking off for no good reason in the middle of a discussion. As for Inès, she needs to mellow. Perhaps arrange a meeting for her with one or two suitors at the end of the day, after one of her long runs in the woods? Fatigue makes her most becoming, veiling her gaze and relaxing her mouth. By clipping their wings, arranging a lock of hair, correcting a facial expression, adjusting their bodies, and persuading them to rein themselves in and be a little more accommodating, Madame Austeur is hopeful of securing a happy future for them. It wouldn't take much, she says to herself, as she closes her notebook.

The governesses love attending the parade of suitors. They simper and put on airs, playing the role of blushing young maidens to great effect. Concealed in the doorway to the smoking room, Monsieur Austeur observes these audiences, stifling a laugh every time they outwit a suitor with their lighthearted banter and rubbing his hands with glee when the poor fellow, so full of hope when he first stepped up, goes off looking downcast. That said, the show they put on has to be seen to be believed. And yet in a house as cut off from the world as theirs is, nothing seems astonishing anymore.

In the three red armchairs the little maids have installed in the main hall they take their seats. Eléonore presides, with Inès on her right and Laura on her left. They're decked out in their finest attire. Eléonore wears a long, tight-fitting, black velvet evening gown with a plunging neckline. Laura, playing the role of a sort of Artemis, is dressed in white silk with a silver satin bow knotted beneath her breasts; glowing in the curls of her hair is a small diamond crescent moon that Madame Austeur has loaned her. Inès is wearing emerald green, with a gemstone on her finger and golden sandals that she's borrowed from one of the maids on her feet.

Throughout the ceremony, in addition to Monsieur Austeur who's hidden from view, you can sense the little maids massed behind the doorway to the salon, and, in the shadows of the round gallery over-looking the hall, the little boys gently craning their necks. So that the elderly gentleman doesn't feel ex-cluded, the door onto the porch has been left open. That way, if he aims his spyglass properly, he'll be able to see into the inner sanctum. As for the brains behind it all, Madame Austeur, she has put on the gray gown she reserves for special occasions, tucked a camellia into her belt, and pinned her wedding brooch over her right breast.

At five o'clock, the suitors file in. Graciously, Ma-dame Austeur greets them on the threshold and, with a discreet sway of the hips you wouldn't have thought she had in her, leads them over to the feet of the governesses. The governesses don't rise. The suitor remains standing and starts to deliver his little speech. Madame Austeur, who has withdrawn a few paces, gently urges him on with a kindly smile. The little maids wriggle around, desperately trying not to laugh. The smoke from Monsieur Austeur's cigar can be seen drifting through the half-open doorway at the end of the hall.

Every now and then, while the suitor is speaking, the governesses stare with the utmost gravity at the area below his belt which seeks to win one of them over. At other moments, they let out a yawn, adjust a shoulder strap, correct the fold of a skirt, or smile at Madame Austeur. They even listen sometimes; and, because they're not made of stone, they're moved. Sensing this, the suitor plucks up courage.

When they're tired of all this playacting, they rise from their thrones, and, with a loud bang that goes echoing through the house, the hall door swings shut. They're back among themselves. They've given themselves a good scare and made everyone's hearts bleed fondly, but all they've really done in pretending to part is to remind themselves how close-knit their ties are and how much bloodshed breaking those ties would cause.

It's not exactly a fiasco, being unable to part. What is the point of parting? To live? And to live where exactly? In a livelier household than their present home? Yet someone in that far-off place would start to resemble Monsieur Austeur, someone else the elderly gentleman, the strangers, the suitors.... Everywhere you'd have the same gates, the same gardens, the same world woven with the same threads connecting a face to a secret room, another face to a second room, and all those scenes they'll never be able to forget but have nevertheless forgotten.

ONE MORNING, LAURA GAVE birth to a child. It didn't come as a surprise exactly, they'd been looking forward to the event for a good nine months now, observing with interest the globe of her belly rounding out beneath her gown. Glowing like the moon, she radiated a sense of peace that the household had never really experienced before.

Laura expectant would come down the steps of the porch, her head nodding gently back and forth like a rubber duck on water, then sit down in the shade of the linden trees while everyone bustled around her, as if preparing for a nativity. Eléonore brought a shawl, Inès a stool, the children flowers. She received these tributes with good grace. She wasn't used to being fussed over in this way. She would smile and look down at her belly without speaking, in order to keep to herself, all to herself, the young life unfolding in her womb. When she was up and walking around, she would fold her pale hands delightedly over the globe of her belly, as though lighting her way in the darkness with an enormous lamp. Monsieur Austeur was quite shaken by the event; Madame Austeur was a little put out that she hadn't been informed earlier. Who had inseminated Laura? Heaven only knows. An audacious suitor? A stranger? The elderly gentleman across the way, breathing into his spyglass as though it were a pipette? The eldest of the little boys? The possibilities, alas, were legion, and the investigation Madame Austeur had entrusted to the little maids turned up nothing. Laura denied having been impregnated by anyone. She had woken up one morning certain that she was expecting a child, that's all there was to it.

If you mentioned a man's name in her presence she would look away, annoyed, so Monsieur Austeur demanded that no further questions be asked of her. Laura was going to be a mother; as for the child's upbringing, it was secure: one day he would join the gaggle of little boys, and that was that.

Which is what happened. After a difficult confinement, Laura discovered a little boy of six pounds lying next to her, a feisty-looking creature, as chubby as you could wish. She was enthralled. She would never have imagined herself capable of such a feat. Secretive by nature, she had always been the last to run to the gates, the last to speak to strangers, the one, she couldn't help thinking, for whom Monsieur Austeur had the least affection and esteem. And yet it was she, the hazy-eyed straggler almost entirely wrapped up in her dreams, who had performed this heroic act, without really knowing how, leaving her two non-childbearing companions far behind her.

It was strange all of a sudden to be running the show, to be the one they all looked up to and turned to for advice. Perhaps that was why she'd had this child: in order to change roles in the household?

She had been moved out of her governess's room, and into the one set aside for young mothers. Situated at the center of the building, it was the largest bedroom in the house and the one with the prettiest decor. Lying in her huge bed with its white quilt and embroidered pillows, she gazed at the freshly laundered net curtains over the tall glass doors leading onto the stone balcony. The creamy white, silk-lined walls and the thick rugs almost entirely covering the parquet made her feel like a jewel in a velvet box. In her new room, the sounds from the house were muffled, unlike in the governesses' rooms, where you could hear ankle boots clicking or Eléonore moaning to herself or Inès splashing in the antiquated pink bathtub. In her new room nobody came bursting in. And when the little maids knocked, they did so by merrily drumming their almond-shaped nails on the wood.

For the first time in her life, Laura was in charge. It wasn't difficult. It was a lot easier than being a governess, where something was always lacking, you were never quite sure what, and couldn't help wondering if, at bottom, it wasn't yourself. She remembered how they'd race over to the gates, their picnics in the forest, the shouts and tears, the strident joys of their life together. It was like remembering her childhood. Those things had happened, no doubt, but all so long ago, in another life, perhaps to a different person ... She no longer dreamed of leaving. The bustle was no longer going on outside; it was here, within the garden, at home, at the center of the house. All you had to do was listen. From time to time, she would part the curtains so that the elderly gentleman across the way could go about his work. But she didn't play with him anymore. No more mincing around, no more striking provocative poses to feel the air vibrating around her. She walked over to her bed and slipped between the sheets—he could watch her dreaming now.

"One less," thought the elderly gentleman to himself as he folded up his telescope. This one wouldn't be wriggling around anymore, this one would never do anything unexpected again. He'd learn nothing more about her from the dress she was wearing, the locks of her hair, her way of pacing up and down. To find a way in, he'd have to look much further afield than her delectable flesh. Stretched out on his bed, with his game of solitaire spread out on the sheets and his big book at his side, he would have to close his eyes.

It was a bit worrying. What if the other two were to marry and leave the house, or, like Laura, give birth to a child—what would become of him and his midnight vigils? Would they simply abandon him one day, after all the joy and hope they had given him? Would he be forced to look out over an enormous, icy garden? He had other distractions, of course: there was his book to examine, the slow procession of the seasons to be followed in the sky and trees; his games of solitaire; the occasional visit perhaps. But these faces he loved, the expressions they wore as they came and went in the garden, which would change suddenly when one of the governesses ran across it—how he would miss it all.... He vowed he would break his telescope in two when the last of the governesses left the stage. He would draw the curtains. He might even pull up stakes and move to another town, another country, and begin afresh. A new life, with no telescope, no standing at the window, no dark room where you conjured up images, darkening or lightening the black parts, adding pink or brown tints to the white bits, playing around with color and form.

No, in his new life he would live. He'd meet other women perhaps, and instead of watching them come and go and rush around, instead of deciphering the mysterious speech on their lips, he would love them in earnest. He would go down to the gardens and terraces, the houses they inhabit, and engage them in conversation. He would untie their ribbons and their bows and unfasten their small pearl buttons. He would run his fingers through their mysterious long hair, touch their lips, put his finger between their teeth.

Because of the governesses, he can't help imagining women in threes. He tries to merge them into a single woman, long and frail, pining for love yet firm as a reed, and at the same time moody. He permits his hands, his mouth, and his sex to explore those moods where they are found, at the junction of the thighs, beneath a thatch of pale summer straw. His fingers slip into moist caverns, make their way up to the soft, sloped belly with its shimmering blonde down, and on up to the tender pale breasts, the tips of which are like everything he ever longed for. And then the frail, willowy neck under a forest of hair. And at last the eyes, the lids fragile as eggshells you can kiss, and the fearless, dreaming brow, the brow that remains so still in the presence of men.

Oh yes, he can see himself living at last. He'll continue to observe her, of course, but she'll observe him, too. She'll call him "darling," or words to that effect. They'll go traveling together, or maybe they'll stay at home — it's really not important. She'll be there with him, he'll be able to touch her, and speak to her as well. He'll wonder how he managed to spend all that time simply watching and listening.

There were times, it's true, when he enjoyed being in his poorly lit room. He loved being tucked up in bed in that warm, dark chamber papered with unicorns and ivy, then pulling out his telescope and snooping in the house and garden. What a delightful way to spend the day! And life was so much less cumbersome, so much less bewildering when kept at bay through that lens. He would watch, write something down in his big book, watch again and write something else down. From time to time, a woman would come in to change the sheets, shake out the pillows, and present him with a crisp, golden-brown roast chicken and a few apples. Then she would disappear.

Did he want to go out sometimes? No, he never felt the urge. He didn't want to be distracted from his task, because that task was the only thing that could make him happy, he knew this perfectly well. Before growing old, he had tried all kinds of things. He had gone out. He, too, had seen the roads and towns. He'd had friends. But he'd never been a good traveler, or a good friend. When he traveled he couldn't wait to get home, and when he spent an evening with friends he couldn't wait to leave. When he was obliged to go out, he was like someone disturbed in a dream and forced to get up in the cold. To go where? He has no idea. He does as he's told, quickly gets to his feet, puts on his clothes, and follows his guide downstairs and out into the road that leads to the bustling, well-lit town. All these lights hurt his eyes and the noises deafen him. He shakes hands, chats, drinks wine, but he still doesn't know what's going on. He's lionized, he is sure he loves his friends, and for a moment he wonders why he doesn't get out more.

And then his guide takes him home, sweating profusely and in a real flap. Everything is colliding in his brain: that lady, the remark she made, the way that man had of snapping his suspenders, the champagne glass he broke, that other woman who seemingly couldn't stand him, the noise. It's too much for him. Too many images and sounds piled together like some horrific car crash. Only one thing from the evening has stuck in his mind, and he clings to it to remain upright: the sound of a bell in a nearby church, reminding him of the governesses.

The further they were from him, the more eager he was to see them again. Everything they'd done while he was away was lost to him forever, and yet he'd come back refreshed. Deprived of their presence for so long, he observed them with a much keener eye than before. Now that he was old, he never went out, except at night, alone, when they were sleeping and the countryside was so still that there was no risk of being distracted from his dreams. He would button himself up in a nice, warm old overcoat, knot a scarf around his neck, thrust his hands into his pockets and, bareheaded, go out for a short stroll along the moonlit road.

How lovely it felt, the chill night air on the crown of your skull.... He turned up the collar of his overcoat and walked softly down the asphalt road, not wanting the tramp of his own feet to disturb him.

There were times when he wasn't alone. One night, he was making his way along the road when silhouettes came creeping up on a path that ran parallel to his own. Hidden by a row of trees, they were obscured from the elderly gentleman's view. In spite of his age, however, he had sharp ears, so when he remarked chirping sounds and stifled laughter, steps scurrying away and a silky rustle of fabric, he felt his heart race like a madman's.

It was the governesses, he was sure. They were

there, in the dark, playing tricks on him. Perhaps they wanted to play? But what did they want him to do exactly? He was worried that he might scare them off. Should he walk faster or carry on at the same pace, as if he hadn't heard anything? Or rush over and pounce on them? Wait on their pleasure, allow them to decide everything? His heart was pounding as he made his way down the gray, moonlit road amid the rustle of leaves and that other, softer and more intimate rustle of the silhouettes who kept him company but had no wish to reveal themselves.

Soon he couldn't hear a sound and felt alarmed. Had they gone? Had they turned back into the woods, leaving him alone until the following morning, when they would reappear on the lawn once more? All of a sudden, he looked up and saw them. Like young deer, they were bounding across the road, one behind the other, a hundred yards in front of him, the folds of their long skirts flying open like wings as they rose, then folding back around their bodies the moment they touched ground.

He started to run, trying to catch up with them, but they had disappeared into the woods. And when he arrived at the spot where they had sailed across the road all he found were a few fallen leaves and the tracks left by their tiny heels in the young grass.

After that night, of course, he went out more often, and always at the same hour and on the same road. He would prick up his ears and think he heard somebody creeping around in the dark, but it was just an animal going by. He heard laughter: it was just water, or pigeons cooing. He scanned the road ahead of him: silhouettes appeared all right, but they didn't leap around and they never rose into the air on outstretched wings. He would come home exhausted from these nocturnal excursions, which became less and less frequent before being phased out altogether. In the morning, it seemed almost miraculous to find the governesses back on the green lawn in their white dresses. Amazed, he observed them closely, filling out their bright, lively forms with night colors, adjusting their contours and silhouettes, advancing.

THE CHILD GREW. SCARVES and little cardigans were knitted for him, and such enormous quantities of miniature socks that no one knew what to do with them. The women in the house were all at it, from Madame Austeur in her white salon, her workbasket at her side, to the little maids unspooling cherry-red and sky-blue balls of wool under the porches. Every time Monsieur Austeur walked through the house, he had the impression of a nest being built. There were scraps of wool everywhere: on the rugs and mantelpieces, dangling from the wainscoting or wound round the banister posts on the stairs. Everywhere he went women would be knitting away without so much as a glance in his direction.

It was starting to get on his nerves. Miniature clothes were piled up on the dressing tables and commodes, and on one occasion he even found a pair of pretty red booties on his desk, which certainly didn't belong there. He lost his temper and called for a semblance of order in the house. He even employed the word "respect." But nobody was listening. They continued to toil away blindly like ants, avoiding him whenever they crossed his path, making him feel like an obstacle, a deadweight, a sort of menhir whose founding role had long been forgotten. So he shut himself away in the smoking room, lonelier than ever. Even his midnight vigils had ceased to serve any real purpose. No one needed him to put them back in orbit anymore, to soothe and direct their sleep. His ministerings were in vain. The center of the house had shifted. It was now located in the room adjoining Laura's on the first floor, behind a cloud of muslin, screaming, crying, laughing, fresh as a baby waterfall.

It was this still unformed voice and consciousness that henceforth regulated the movements of the household. To Monsieur Austeur it came as a shock. What! His age and experience and all the hardships he had endured could simply be usurped by this tiny creature with next to no knowledge of life? Was the child's arrival in the world really enough to dethrone him—he who, on account of his age and experience and the hardships he had endured, had always felt entitled to run the house? It was as though his whole life up to that point had been weighed on some strange scale and judged of no more worth than the featherweight of existence enjoyed by this piddling little infant.

Madame Austeur could sense her husband's confusion. She would have liked to come to his aid but had herself been swept up like a wisp of straw on this powerful new tide, and had no sooner turned to him with open arms than she disappeared from view, as though swallowed up by the room on the second floor.

Had the governesses been more thoughtful, they might have shown him more respect. But what a fool he had been to count on their support! They no more knew what they were doing than Madame Austeur did; as tenderhearted as the little maids, they sank down in this ocean of softness, bouncing happily around in a kind of zero gravity.

And to think he'd expected them to rally round at the first puff of smoke from his cigar! That, whatever the circumstance, whatever the temptations, it was to him they would turn, him they would support with their powerful young love.

Wounded, Monsieur Austeur spent more and more time out of doors: in the orchard, where he would clip the trees; in town, where he suddenly had things to do; or on long walks that led nowhere and only brought him back to a house where life had withdrawn to a spot that was out of bounds to him.

Nobody prevented him from entering that room, and yet he couldn't help tiptoeing past it, removing his shoes on the landing when he came in late. And were the door to start to open while he was standing there, he would hurry back to his living quarters, hugging the walls like a burglar, without once finding the slender, austere silhouette of Madame Austeur waiting there to console him.

The spectacle now confronting him astonished him: Madame Austeur in a red dress, bounding up and down the stairs four steps at a time and singing like an opera star. He would hear her laughter cascading through the hall. She never used to laugh like that, not even during their engagement when, though she was shy, it's true, she could be so youthful and accommodating, and even cooing, at times. She worshipped him in those days, her eyes would light up when he proposed a walk or picked up a little feather on the lawn and offered it to her. She was as delighted by the feather he gave her as she was by his love. And it was because of this happiness that he loved her. With her, the house would be gay and lighthearted. The windows would always be wide open, the curtains would flutter in the breeze, and even in winter it would be so mild and merry outside that the great marbled hall would be like an ice rink where she would glide around on her little feet, speeding toward him with flushed pink cheeks and slightly tousled hair as he held out his arms to her. With age Madame Austeur had become less gay. Was it that he loved her less? That he didn't give her enough pleasure or gave it clumsily? Yet she didn't seem to desire that pleasure anymore.... And so they moved to a different circle—together and hand in hand, but a little sadly, as though turning their backs on something they had vowed to accomplish and had been unable to attain.

This was when they started to lie to each other. Oh, nothing serious, of course: they merely hid their souls from each other slightly. They would try not to, but whenever they rushed toward each other it was as though their souls came up against an invisible obstacle and they would fall back to earth before they could unite. They felt humiliated by these falls, as an old man does when he gets to his feet thinking he can walk and his legs give way beneath him. They never spoke of these intimate defeats.

And so the lies accumulated, like links in a chain. So much so that there came a time when they were telling each other nothing but lies. It had become their new life. They didn't much like staring into each other's eyes in silence, but as this was easy enough to avoid, they overcame that final hurdle in no time at all. Their life was an exact replica of what it had been before, only the other way round. There was even a rekindling of their passion during this period: it was such a relief not to have to struggle anymore.

They could have tried to break out of this new circle, of course. But at what cost? The thought made them shudder. Madame Austeur would probably have left the house. Or Monsieur Austeur. And neither could imagine living without the other. They preferred to go on lying to each other. They preferred to live apart, so long as they were together. And that wasn't so simple either. It's not that easy to keep one's soul under lock and key, as it were. It was like being alone in the world and, in a way, doomed. Yet they were in thrall to a kind of law according to which the person who has accompanied you in love will be the one who accompanies you in death. They were like animals, obedient to an instinct whose meaning and function eluded them.

It was at this point that they hired the governesses. The moment they walked through the golden gates, Monsieur and Madame Austeur knew that it was all over between them; they would have to start playing a different game.

WHEN THE CHILD WAS introduced to the group of little boys, he was welcomed like a king. They would fall over each other to offer him the finest fruits, the prettiest silver fish caught in the river, to show him the "hideaway" behind the greenhouse or point out the spot in the corner of the kitchen garden where the gooseberry bushes grew.

While the child staggered around, collapsing in a heap on top of the ducklings he'd try to catch like a cat chasing its shadow in the mirror, the governesses followed behind, splitting their sides with laughter as they reached down to prevent him from falling or to push a branch or the handle of a wheelbarrow out of the way.

Such a fuss was made of the child that there were times when he seemed slightly overwhelmed by it all. He would plop down on his little padded bottom, clench his fists, and let out a howl while dogs circled round sniffing at him and turkeys waddled over.

Since recovering from her lying-in, Laura seemed almost to have forgotten what had happened to her, delegating her responsibilities as a mother so readily to the other women in the household that Madame Austeur was shocked. She tried to knock a bit of sense into the absentminded governess, but Laura wasn't listening. She was happy to roam back and forth on her own all day, drifting around, chewing on a blade of grass. It was as if her former life had taken possession of her again, but even more firmly and artfully than in the past.

The child would sit crying among the turkeys, and Laura wouldn't even glance over. He would wake in his cot, but she had already gone out, tramping around since dawn. And when she returned, instead of going up to his room she would linger on the porch with the little maids or stand at a window, gazing out at the garden.

She believed she had put that life behind her while lying up in the huge white bed at the center of the house. But little by little, in that very room, she had fallen back into her old ways. At the moment of birth she had felt like a violin, a vessel that had been split down the middle. From her had sprung this little creature already miraculously formed, singular, unknown. Then the sides of the vessel had slipped quietly back into place and nothing remained of the opening. When she placed her hand there she found it mute, and so similar to what it had been before that it was as though she'd been dreaming. Then she heard crying or babbling in the next room, rose from her bed, walked through to the other room, and bent over the cradle. In it was someone unknown crying out for her care but, in all important respects, already equipped for life.

She felt a kind of love for him, a strange, giddying tenderness. Yet it was as if the child had chosen to be born in her rather than she to bear him, and she couldn't understand the mystery of that choice. Why her, rather than one of the others? What was being asked of *her*, Laura? They looked into each other's eyes, she questioning him, he responding to her gaze with the lake of his eyes. There was something ancient about him, as though he had sprung from between her bleeding thighs after a long journey. She felt very small and very young in his presence, ignorant. Didn't she have something to learn from him? When he looked at her, it reminded her of other gazes: the last glance of a dying man, or the look of a man who loves you and must leave you. It was a farewell, of that she was certain.

And so it was, for the creature would grow into a baby. A laughing, crying, thirsty, hungry little thing, who instead of an ancient gaze had the youthful gaze of a baby. He was no longer the creature full of space and time she had borne into the world, he was someone else. The other had gone forever.

That was why Laura had grown mournful and started to roam around on her own. She had lost someone. She grieved for the figure who had vanished in a matter of days to be replaced by a different one, one who was fresh and new. It was the other figure she loved. The one who had chosen to be born in her and had said so through the lake of his gaze, and whose body of knowledge had vanished in a matter of days.

She mulled the matter over as she walked alone, telling herself that she, too, in that case, must have chosen the cradle of her fate. What was it, then, that she had pledged to do? And had she done it? Was she doing it now? She viewed the gardens in a different light, the tops of the young trees in a different light, Eléonore and Inès with curiosity. Suddenly it all made sense, it all had a purpose. And she became lost in thought, forgetting to care for the child, engrossed in her own birth, which had followed so closely on that of her child.

But even that didn't last. Impressions spring up,

for a time alter your body temperature slightly, and then fall away, blending so completely into your flesh that nothing remains. Laura gobbled up the powerful impression the birth of her child had made on her. Just as the intimate gap in her belly had closed again after the child appeared and was today as intact as if nothing had ever happened, so her spirit, after opening for a moment, had folded its wings. It was the old Laura once more, the one with her head in the clouds, the slowest of the three when it came to running to the gates or plunging into the woods with a throbbing heart in pursuit of God knows what.

Eléonore and Inès were surprised to find her restored to her former self. They asked her to tell them about the lying-in, the sensations she had felt, sure of hearing extraordinary revelations. Laura's words—hesitant, vague—disappointed them.

After a while, the child joined the group of little boys and soon became hard to tell apart from the others. He had the same hair, the same eyes, the same cries of delight, the same quick little legs that raced up and down the stairs ten times a day. Like them he rolled a hoop, like them he unhitched the ponies and went trundling across the lawns, like them he slept in the attic, daydreamed in the greenhouse, sucked on the pistils of flowers.

Nothing, then, had changed. What bomb would need to be dropped on the house for life to change all of a sudden? For the gates to fly open and the up-rooted trees and displaced house to form a different landscape?

The elderly gentleman had returned to his window, happy and at the same time a little disappointed. So he wouldn't be leaving after all. There would be no new life. And holding up his spyglass, he turned his back on the lithe new woman and the love he would have felt for her, her way of saying the word "darling," their travels together in those distant lands.

Once more they were jumping around on the lawns, soliciting his gaze and signaling to him, clapping their hands when they discovered the reflection of his telescope once more playing over their dresses and the wall of the house, or climbing into the trees like a butterfly in summer.

With the little boys, they larked about chasing after the reflection, trying to catch it, slapping their hands down over their skirts or a windowpane. Then, all of a sudden, they would pretend to have caught it, and when the little boys huddled round in a circle, curious to see, they would quickly part their hands and, at the same instant, the elderly gentleman would angle his spyglass in such a way that the little boys saw a blond flame flying up. Dazzled by this new marvel on the part of the governesses, they gazed up into the sky, while the younger boys rushed off into the house and up the staircase to try and catch the reflection on the roof, as though going to flush out a bird.

By the time they reached the roof, the reflection had vanished. They searched everywhere for it, rummaging through the trunks in the attic, then running their hands along the gutter on the hunch that the birds might have gobbled it up and spat it out again. Only at nightfall did their treasure hunt come to an end.

They dreamed about it. It was as though there was a mystery in the house, something hidden that, from time to time, would reveal itself so that they could look for it, then disappear again just when they were getting warm. It was there somewhere, the reflection, but where? And how could you catch it before it flew away? They armed themselves with butterfly nets and boxes pierced with small holes, and stealthily, speaking in whispers, spent whole days combing through the house, accidentally knocking over a vase at the bottom of which they thought they had glimpsed the reflection and frightening the little maids when they clapped their nets over their heads all of a sudden—and then, with a great fanfare, trailing triumphantly out onto the lawn.

The older boys turned their noses up at all this

excitement. They wouldn't be caught dead taking part in one of these hunts. But sometimes, as they strolled around the gardens with their superior airs, they would glance round suddenly at a fleeting glint of light and feel their hearts pounding.

FROM TIME TO TIME, the governesses go off on long treks and disappear into the heather. For three days, nobody sees them. It's not that they're outdoor types, or even that they have a passionate love of nature. As we have seen, they do everything by fits and starts and never carry anything through to completion—except Laura, perhaps, in giving birth to her child. A hundred times, for example, they have vowed to learn Latin or Hebrew. They take lessons for two or three days, then all of a sudden a word, a tree glimpsed through the window, a dream they had the night before distracts them, somehow requires all their attention, and they stop studying so that they can daydream. Or else they decide to take up botany and wildlife, buy books and herbariums and consult dictionaries, then two days later they're their old selves again. It's as though the channel they seek for their lives has been present all along, but buried so deep and so hidden from view that they can never position themselves there by thinking, only by a sort of yielding. When they're idle, they feel much closer to the riverbed than when they're busy and determined. An obscure sense of guilt, however, forces them to act from time to time. "Let's go hiking," they say, "let's explore nature, look at trees and flowers, we'll bring back a harvest of new impressions which we can examine at leisure when we get home."

Their bodies jump around in the heather. They've left the little boys back at the house and are having a few days off. Here there's a hazel tree where the hazelnuts are too green and taste bitter; over there, some cows looking round at them, whom they wave at cheerfully. A yapping dog comes skipping over, accompanies them as far as an invisible boundary, then stops dead in his tracks. They've seen so many different landscapes in this region: waterlogged spring meadows filled with the sound of burbling streams, moorlands of grass and water with wild daffodils shooting up everywhere; gorse bushes flowering under a stark, cold blue sky, while they pound the dry earth with their feet, their hands sunk deep in their pockets; in late summer, blackberry bushes that make your fingers bleed and hedgerows of sour pink

92

red-currants clustered together beneath tender green leaves.

They've been living with Monsieur and Madame Austeur for so long now that they've swallowed up all these impressions and images, possessed them a thousand times over. And yet they've never felt it was enough to live on. It was like the first intimation of happiness, or rather, the precise note struck by happiness. By listening carefully, they try to make their life resemble that sound.

Hiking around like this, they experience the kind of joy that makes you eager for life, and eager to lead a fuller life. Whenever they walked past a leafy green enclosure they felt, not that happiness was there in that leafy green enclosure, in the shade of the thick oak trees, but that happiness was like that, had the silent majesty of those leaves, the dimensions of that buoyant enclosure, the dreamy depths of its carpet of grass, and that they needed to have all these forces and qualities coursing through their life.

Then there were the late autumn landscapes when everything gently decays, when wood mixes with the earth and water turns leaves into a russet pulp. Yielding to those laws, the governesses would allow their impressions of summer to mingle together and grow heavy. They would sit passively by the fireside, as though going to meet their death, feeding their forthcoming spring with this fuming dung heap weighing heavily inside them like a witch's brew. Then winter set in, season of bones and skeletons. They read prayer books, honed their souls, enclosed their bodies in long mourning robes, grew pale, barely ate a thing.

The arrival of spring called for a celebration. At the first scent of April, when space seems to expand all of a sudden and become as airy and light as a bubble, they would put on their pale green dresses and run to the gates. In the kisses they exchanged with strangers, the whole of the previous summer, and the whole of autumn and winter could be found. They were frenzied kisses, unrestrained and overflowing with mystic thoughts. Kisses that contained — as though in little cases — the sweltering heat and sweating bodies, the screaming red flesh of summer; the decay and weight and fumes of autumn; the slender, black mineral forms of winter. The strangers were taken aback. They took another taste of the governesses' mouths and found all the seasons there. They seized on their lips and pink tongues, ran their fingers over their pearly white teeth. It was flowers they were biting into, rivers they were drinking, which is why they felt so powerful after kissing them. When the governesses put their dresses back on and smoothed their collars and hair with the flat of their hand, the men thought them heartless and felt abandoned.

In the course of their excursions, the governesses would stretch out in the long grass or tumble headlong down an entire mountain meadow. They loved to climb trees, feel their legs being cut to ribbons and their muscles working. They bathed in streams where the cold water gripped you like a fist, chewed on the stems of flowers and stroked their faces with clumps of pink grass. Everything was a delight to them— stubbing their foot on a stone, tearing their flesh on thorn bushes, feeling the venomous soft caress of stinging nettles on their calves. At times they would have liked to rub the nettles all over their bodies.

Did they come back from their excursions in one piece? Oh, never! They would come back like true travelers, after almost freezing to death, getting burned, cutting themselves on the razor-sharp grass and bleeding, bleeding.... Had they been younger, they would have wallowed in the mud and smeared it all over their bodies. But they weren't twenty anymore and drew a line at certain forms of behavior. They climbed naked into the trees, of course. They needed to feel the rough, gnarled skin of tree trunks against their tender breasts, their tender bellies, their tender thighs, just as they needed to bathe naked in the icy water that made their hearts leap. When they were up to their necks in the water, they would close their eyes, and their bodies, as though anesthetized, would fly overhead, winging their way across the sky and on into the firmament. All that remained was their heads, resting on the surface of the stream like water lilies.

The moment they emerged from its icy fist, their bodies came back to life. To warm them, they would rub them so hard that they turned bright pink. Then they would lash themselves with twigs and, streaked with crimson welts, race along the riverbank, clutching their breasts and giving off so much heat that a mist would form around them, accompanying them as they ran.

In autumn, what they most enjoyed was the smell of leaves softened by the rain. They would lie down with their bellies to the earth, bury their faces in a mulch of red and black leaves, rub their cheeks in them, then inhale deeply like a dog sniffing at a scent. They loved to feel the rain flooding their bodies and would prolong their walks until they were soaked through, arriving home with their hair all over the place and their eyes on fire.

Madame Austeur didn't really like seeing them in this state. It was as though they had been at a witches' sabbath or something of that sort. The governesses seemed so alien to her at moments like these that they might have torn her to pieces with their teeth or flown straight up to the second floor in the whirl-wind of their boiling robes.

Fearful, she hid in the small salon and watched them through the half-open door as they passed along the hall.

They climbed the stairs as if cleaving through water, gripped the banister as though about to start dancing, raced upstairs, then back down again, quite oblivious to their supernumerary powers, which were far too potent for a single household, too nimble of foot for a single flight of stairs, and so ardent that the mere electricity of their presence was enough to set the curtains ablaze. And when they went to close the shutters of their room, it was only by clutching on to them that they were prevented from being caught up in their own slipstream and flying out the win-dow. The world had become Lilliputian to them, the house a doll's house, the gardens a Japanese garden of the kind you concoct with children on rainy days, making trees out of twigs, rocks with three bits of gravel, a lake in a saucer, and casting caterpillars in the role of enormous prehistoric monsters.

That's how the world looked to them when they came back from one of their excursions. With one hand they would pluck bunches of trees from the gar-den, folding them flat against the grass then snapping them off at the base of the stem; with the other, they would lift off the roof of the house and take hold of a distraught Madame Austeur or one of the little maids between thumb and forefinger. At the end of his telescope, the elderly gentleman would discover a leg like the tower of Babel or a breast the size of a heavenly sphere. In this new landscape — where there were woods, plains, mountains and streams, and a few tangled creepers — he was quite lost and would wonder where the governesses had gone. Then all of a sudden, on a clear day, he would see their gigantic heads high above him. Laura would be sticking her tongue out at him — an enormous fiery tongue, like a red carpet unfurling from the heavens. He would plop down on it, the tongue would quickly roll up, and lo! like Jonas he would fall into the governess's gullet and belly. It was a huge pink echo chamber, like the inside of an ear or a seashell. He would lie down there, a tiny old man in a nice, warm overcoat, with his scarf knotted around his neck. He would lie there flat on his back, his hands cupped behind his head, happy as a lark, smiling to himself and gazing up at the sky and stars, for in this pink belly there would be some form of sky and stars. From time to time, he would stand up and, shading his eyes with his hand, search for the horizon; but try as he might, he could see no end to the belly. It was infinite.

Then their excitement falls abruptly away, like a

dress dropping to the ground when the straps are loosened. Their gargantuan stature lies stranded at their feet, like a sagging hot-air balloon. When they crawl out from underneath this sea of fabric, they're stark naked and very small. It's the house now that starts to swell, to the point where they're suddenly the size of puppies, and then, in no time at all, ducklings. They waddle through the enormous rooms, getting knocked around by the young maids' feet, and the windows are so high that they can't see the sky, they feel trapped. It takes them hours to get downstairs, and what a business that is, too. When the doors are closed, how will they be able to open them? The doorknobs are far too high and impossible to turn. They blunder around, it takes them days to find their way back to their rooms. In the garden, right before their eyes, is a huge savannah. There aren't even gates on the horizon anymore. Then they return to their normal size.

WHEN THE GOVERNESSES WERE twenty and cooing under the trees, the little boys were crazy about them. Whenever one of the little boys drew a face, it was theirs, whenever one of them wondered what he might do to please people later in life, all he had to do was imagine himself under the watchful eye of the governesses.

Left to their own devices much of the time, the little boys formed a sort of fourth section in the house. First, you had Monsieur and Madame Austeur who, because they shared the same room, were bound together and formed a single unit. Next, you had the little maids who, because they all slept in the attic, were also bound together by having identical rooms. And last, but by no means least, you had the governesses who, though less powerful than Monsieur and Madame Austeur combined, were much more powerful than the little maids and likewise formed a single unit.

These four sections were bound together, at different moments in time and in no particular order, in batches of two. Some of the little boys found these shifts of alliance very hard to follow, for they would occur without any real warning. They would get in a muddle and have to use all their powers to find the right match. Sometimes, for example, the governesses would mysteriously and inexplicably be paired for a while with the little maids. When that happened, it was important to understand that the governesses had no time to look after you, and that your plant collections, however beautifully assembled, inspired nothing but a big yawn. Foolishly, the little boys would imagine the governesses had lost all interest in their collections, perhaps even in the little boys themselves. It was tough, but they got used to it after a while. They found ways to console themselves, piecing together as best they could a small new life shorn of the governesses' love but tolerable just the same. Then, all of a sudden, without warning, the alliances would change. This time it was the little boys who were teamed up with the governesses. Once again they had to pull out their herbariums and show them to the governesses, who would clap their hands in delight and now seemed to dote on them, while the little maids sobbed away in their attic rooms.

They would just be getting used to the governesses' love again—it didn't take very long to reacquire the habit, it was so easy to sink back into their love—when all of a sudden Monsieur and Madame Austeur would regain the upper hand. You would see them strolling through the garden with the governesses; they'd spend whole evenings chatting and laughing together, just the five of them. Under the circumstances, the only thing the little boys could do was form an alliance with the little maids, in order to balance things out, as it were. At the same time, they blushed at the idea of being teamed up with them. Not that they thought the little maids inferior in any way—on the whole, they had the most fun with them—but they would have preferred to choose their allies, rather than fall back on whoever was left over for them.

As they were proud, the boys would pretend they had made their choice of their own free will, lavishing a great show of affection on the little maids, who henceforth imagined they were loved by them and figured prominently in their airy young lives. And when the roles changed yet again—not because of anything done by the little boys, who weren't powerful enough to influence the movements of the household, but for reasons that remain mysterious—the little maids, cruelly cast aside, would feel betrayed in their trust, while the little boys, who were quicker off the mark, would rush into the first set of arms held out to them, regardless of what group they might belong to.

It was like musical chairs. There was always someone left on their own while the others struck up alliances, friendships that would last a lifetime perhaps. Experience had shown you, however, that no pact lasts forever. You knew that the members of the household would once again be shuffled together like playing cards, and that when the next hand was dealt the alliances would fall out differently. There might even be a place for you. But how could you be sure a new hand would be dealt? Perhaps this was the final hand, and henceforth everyone would be stuck in the place that fate had assigned them? Still, you had to be on your guard, just in case, one last time, the bonds were broken and new ones formed. At which point you would have to quickly rush over to the right side.

The governesses had teamed up with the little maids of late. They formed a gracious scene, seated in their flared skirts under the high trees, sewing and gossiping. The little boys felt abandoned, but lingered nearby, dawdling, hardly playing at all and not taking their eyes off them. At the slightest hint of a change—were the governesses to stop talking to the little maids, say, or yawn in a supercilious way—they would creep up, ready to pounce and take the little maids' place. But, often as not, the change that a moment before had seemed imminent never occurred: the governesses would start chatting with the little maids again, holding their balls of wool for them or playing with their hair.

The alliance the little boys least enjoyed was the one with Monsieur and Madame Austeur. It made them a bit uneasy, as though they were falling into line and doing what was expected of them. It was much more dangerous and exciting to be teamed up with the governesses. And even with the little maids there was something voluptuous about feeling yourself bound together by some strange perversity of fate. In attaching yourself to Monsieur and Madame Austeur, you couldn't help feeling that, though reason might be on your side, it was on the other side that you had all the fun.

With Monsieur and Madame Austeur they were like those model children you see strolling around with their model parents. The parents are happy, but the children feel ashamed. They would rather resemble one of those mysterious courting couples who walk by without noticing them. When strolling around with their model parents, model children see everything. Their eyes look outward, they're not remotely interested in the spectacle of the family; they pretend to be no part of it, bond immediately with any stranger who happens along and follow him. The shame they feel is further exacerbated by the fact that their parents don't even realize they have escaped. If only their parents would lose their temper once in a while! Demand that they be there with them and nowhere else! Then perhaps they would snuggle up in the bosom of the family, glad to belong there in the end, now that the battle is over. But what makes them so ashamed is the model parents' blind trust, their self-delusion. They'd like to feel sorry for them in their blindness, but they can't. It's abhorrent to see them so sound asleep.

So when the little boys are in a group with Monsieur and Madame Austeur, they pretend they have chosen the alliance of their own free will. A bit like with the little maids, but for different reasons. It's certainly not for Monsieur and Madame Austeur's benefit that they keep up the pretense, it's for the eyes of the world—for themselves, in other words.

The alliance they most enjoy, of course, is the one they form with the governesses. With them, they feel empowered; with them, they can come and go as they please, screaming their heads off and run-

ning wild through the gardens, lashing the high grass
and any flower that raises its unassuming head. But
though that alliance is flattering to them and opens
up thrilling new paths to explore, they're still not
completely satisfied with it. At the end of the day,
they can't help feeling, it's all just make-believe.

No, what they prefer more than anything, though
they would never admit to it for fear of looking a bit
soppy, is their extramural alliance with the elderly
gentleman. It's in his orbit that they feel their best.
Not like little boys, as they do with Monsieur and
Madame Austeur, nor like savages as they do with
the little maids, nor torn by a thousand misgivings
as they do with the governesses, but in their rightful
place, calm and full of self-respect, and at the same
time brimming with life.

Sometimes, to give the governesses a rest and keep
up good neighborly relations with Monsieur and Madame Austeur, the elderly gentleman takes the little
boys for a walk. They stroll cheerfully around him,
chasing butterflies and only too happy to follow in
the wake of the overcoat in which the elderly gentleman is wrapped as he marches calmly, steadily on.

If anyone can be said to be the little boys' friend,
it's the elderly gentleman. With him you can be a
numbskull or a sissy, cry because you've sprained
your ankle, talk about girls, hum a word you're fond

of a hundred times over even if it's a rude one, say nothing and go about your little life, or march solemnly at the head of the group, your neck wrapped in the elderly gentleman's scarf and waving a branch around like a flag.

You don't have to bend over backwards to please the elderly gentleman, not at all. Whether you bend over backwards or are a bit of a clumsy dolt, he speaks to you and looks at you in exactly the same way. He doesn't say much, but when he does speak he stays on his side of the fence, which obliges you to stay on yours. What's strange, even miraculous in a way, is that when you all stay on your own side of the fence you manage to get on much better than in circumstances where you have to step out of your own skin, as it were, and inhabit someone else's world; or, conversely, when someone gets it into their head to pay you a visit and comes in through a passageway you're not so sure you wanted to unlock for them.

The elderly gentleman, for all his great age, is an equal. He doesn't lead you on a mad dance like the governesses. He lets you go at your own good speed. And on days when he himself, it seems, is feeling unusually cheerful and goes striding on ahead, he couldn't care less whether you chase along behind him or not. He's glad you're there, that's all there is to it.

There came a day, however, when, much to everyone's surprise, the elderly gentleman withdrew, for
he was tired of watching the governesses. They could
sense this from the fall in the number of reflections
in the garden, of shadows outside their bedroom
windows. It didn't worry them at first: they were so
accustomed to being watched that they gave it no
thought except when playing; the rest of the time,
they behaved as though the elderly gentleman didn't
exist. Perhaps it was this that had annoyed or upset
him in the end—who knows? One day, he went up
to the window overlooking the garden and drew the
curtains. For a few days, he remained in a comforting
half dark, then parted the curtains to the other window, the one overlooking the countryside behind his
house. Henceforth, it was here that he would position himself with his telescope. The first objects he
saw were a fern leaf and a hare.

A few days later, despite the continued presence
of Monsieur and Madame Austeur and the little boys
and little maids, the governesses started to feel dis-
tinctly queasy. It was almost as if they were disappearing. They looked puzzled, examined themselves
in the mirrors, and darted questioning glances at each
other without knowing quite what it was they were
asking. "We're fading," announced Eléonore one
day. "We're melting away," replied Laura. Worried,

Inès went down to the garden and started striding toward the gates. She was still on the path when she vanished. The gardens shrank, the little boys toppled over, the house lost its walls, Monsieur Austeur his cigar, Madame Austeur her gray dress, the little maids the platters they had been carrying. In place of Eléonore was a small flower between two pebbles; where Laura had been standing, a lizard darting away.